CW01159869

GAINING PERSPECTIVE

Lessons I'm Learning from Taylor

David M. Kantor

Copyright © 2010 David M. Kantor.
All rights reserved.

ISBN: 1450559964
ISBN-13: 9781450559966
Library of Congress Control Number: 2010901569

This book is dedicated to my amazing wife, Leslie. I am so lucky to have you to help me care for Taylor.

It's also dedicated to my other three daughters, Tiffany, Tatum, and Jayda. They all love Taylor unconditionally and protect her at all costs.

And of course, this book is dedicated to Taylor, without whom I would be a much shallower person and so much less inspired.

Table of Contents

Chapter 1   Listen 1

Chapter 2   Reach Out 4

Chapter 3   Do What's Expected of You 7

Chapter 4   Accept Good Intentions 10

Chapter 5   Your Possessions 12

Chapter 6   Don't Try to Control Others . . . 15

Chapter 7   Be True to Yourself 17

Chapter 8   Remember People's Names . . . 24

Chapter 9   Perspective on Diet 26

Chapter 10 Watch What You Do to Yourself . . .28

Chapter 11 Experience Love 30

Chapter 12 Encourage Others 33

Chapter 13 Learn Patience 35

Chapter 14 Exceed Your Limitations Every Day. .37

Gaining Perspective

LESSONS I'M LEARNING FROM TAYLOR
FOURTEEN KEYS TO A BETTER, HAPPIER,
AND MORE FULFILLED LIFE!

At age forty-four, I had, by measure of most Americans, a great deal of success. I had (and still have) a loving twenty-three-year marriage to my college sweetheart and a diamond business I had founded on a shoestring and built to a multimillion dollar corporation. I had (and still have) four gorgeous daughters who were (and are) happy and fulfilled (if not a bit spoiled), and I had many material possessions: A 5,000-plus-square-foot home in a gated community in Rancho Mirage (a wealthy southern California resort town); a second home that is over 3,800 square feet on the water in my hometown, Gig Harbor, Washington, where we spend our summers; a condo in Seattle; a Lexus; a motorcycle; and my wife and two of our daughters all had brand new cars. Over the course of our marriage, we had owned BMWs, a Mercedes, a Hummer, a Volvo, a Jaguar, and a Corvette. We had flat-screen TVs, new computers, kayaks for playing in the water, country club memberships, golf carts, a swimming pool, etc. I realized how fortunate we were. But something wasn't quite right, and I never felt truly happy. There were arguments with my wife, fights with my children, and constant arguments with vendors, advertising partners, and employees of my businesses. I never felt like I was in the right place.

Then things started to become challenging. My wife and I came close to separating, my business volume was going backward, and former employees were suing me. All that had been tolerable because I was making plenty of money and had lots of things, started to become intolerable. I started to seek answers.

For many years, I had taken long walks with my oldest daughter, Taylor, who is what most people would consider severely disabled. I would push her in her oversized jogger, and we would go for three to eight miles and *talk*. That is, I would talk, and

Taylor would listen attentively because she can't speak. Everyone who knew that I did this would ask about the walks, and I would always jokingly say that on the walks, Taylor and I would solve all our problems. I'd say that I took Taylor on walks because she was so good at helping me work out the solutions to challenges in my life. Everyone would have a laugh, and that would be it.

But then I started thinking, maybe Taylor does hold the keys to answering most of my questions. She is the most unique and different person I know—why couldn't she help me? Things always seemed okay, and most of my worries and anger would melt away when I was with Taylor. I started analyzing Taylor—where she was in the world, how she related to people and problems, and how they related to her. All of the sudden, *lessons* started coming from Taylor. Of course, she wouldn't verbalize them, she merely responded to things, issues, and care, and the lessons would come to me. I started frantically looking for pens and scraps of paper all the time. Things came to me in fits and starts. At long last, I figured out Taylor's purpose in life—to teach lessons on perspective and to help people (or at the very least, me) learn how to relate to others and their challenges.

As you can see by the title, I say I'm "learning" these lessons. By no means have I mastered the perspective that Taylor has taught me nor do I remember to always use that perspective in my daily life. I'm simply a student of Taylor's perspective, and every day, I try hard to live up to her standards.

This book may seem simplistic in its approach and some of its teachings. That's one of the lessons on gaining perspective from Taylor. For things to work and be effective, they most often should be simple, easy, and without extra filling.

It is my sincere hope that the readers of this book will gain the perspective they need in their lives to deal with whatever issues seem to be challenging them.

David M. Kantor
Taylor's first perspective student

CHAPTER 1

Listen

Listen intently. Taylor cannot speak. Her muscle weakness doesn't allow her to utilize her mouth the way you are so fortunate to be able to. Taylor can hear, and not only does she hear, but she listens. I can always tell when Taylor is listening intently because she either turns her head to one side and looks at me, or she gets very excited, waving her arms, kicking her legs, and shaking her head from side to side.

Taylor listens intently because it's one of the few things she can do well (by "normal" standards). She simply cannot speak. But how often do you listen intently? Most of us (myself included) are obsessed with:
- Getting our point across.
- Drowning out opposition to our opinions.

- Being considered smart or charismatic.
- Making sure things go our way.

But how can we learn anything by speaking? We can't. So many people have so many interesting and helpful things to teach us. We don't hear them because we don't listen.

I can assure you that, after twenty-one years of silence, if Taylor began to speak, there wouldn't be anything or anyone that would be more important to those that know and love Taylor than what she had to say. We would listen with rapt attention, hanging on every word.

There isn't one person in my family who hasn't had the dream that Taylor spoke to them. It's always varied, but the dream would be something along the lines of Taylor secretly telling one person in the family that she could speak and she was only going to talk to them. Believe me, everyone who had that dream was so interested in what Taylor had to say, that when they woke up, they rushed to find out if it was real. Unfortunately, it wasn't. Taylor can't speak.

But most everyone you come across in your daily life has something of value to share. If they are your kids, nothing is more special to them than telling you their thoughts, their dreams, their goals, and their disappointments.

Do you listen intently to your children? Your spouse? Your extended family? Your business associates? Your employees? I know I didn't. But I gained perspective from Taylor, and I try to now listen intently whenever possible. You know what? It's a lot more inspiring, interesting, and enriching than speaking!

CHAPTER 2

Reach Out
Greet someone—
No Matter the Response

I'm not naturally outgoing. Most people aren't. So it's no surprise that most people keep to themselves:
1. From their normal preference
2. For fear of the response.

But every morning, I say, "Good morning!" to Taylor. Every morning I ask, "How you feelin' today?" Every day I ask her, "Are you going to have a good day today?" Guess what the response is? Silence. But she usually smiles, and that's all I need to know I've made a difference in her day.

For twenty-one-plus years I've gone outside my normal nature to heartily greet, question, and encourage someone who never responds in kind. Why? Because if I didn't start the conversation, no one would. If I didn't, or my wife Leslie didn't, or Taylor's sisters or others didn't, Taylor would never be spoken to.

How many times have you said "hello," "good morning," "how's it going?" or simply smiled at someone and gotten no response? What was your response to that? Most likely it's something along the lines of, "What a _____!" (Fill in the derogatory remark.) Or you thought, "That's the last time I'm going to reach out again," and became even more introverted.

But that's the wrong reaction. If I stopped trying to dialogue with Taylor when I didn't get a verbal response, I would have stopped speaking to her a long time ago. It's my job to start the conversation and attempt to exchange pleasantries no matter the response.

It's your job to do the same, to whomever you encounter. It's your job to try to make someone's day better and to speak to someone who maybe has no one else talking to them in their lives. No matter if the person (or the first five people) you encounter every day ignores your pleasantries—reaching out will make you feel better. At some point, you'll get a great response: a happy smile; you may even make the difference in changing a person's day, week, or view of life.

There are lots of people like Taylor, not disabled but unable, for whatever reason, to respond to your kindness, but they'll be more appreciative of your action than you'll ever know.

CHAPTER 3

Do What's Expected of You

Everyone has a job to do. Everyone has family members who rely on them for some reason or another. Everyone is a member of society and is expected to do their part.

But how many people go out of their way to shirk their responsibilities? They try to get by with the least amount of effort and don't ever think of offering help unless asked or even begged. That would be most people.

I don't have that option with Taylor. She expects me to help her in the morning, to change her clothes and diaper, to feed her, brush her teeth, to wash her face. She's there, every day, expecting these things. There are no shortcuts with Taylor. I have no choice but to live up to or exceed her expectations of me. If I didn't, then she'd quite literally die.

But when I'm with Taylor, something amazing happens. Most people who would pass me without a second thought, always give Taylor a knowing smile. They hold doors open. They stop their cars to allow us to pass. They even offer to lift her and/or her chair.

We were in New York one year for Thanksgiving. The night of Thanksgiving, we were going to a restaurant about three blocks from our hotel. It started to rain. Now with Taylor being medically fragile, she can't be out in that weather for long without getting sick. So I was going to run ahead with Taylor to the restaurant to get her out of the rain (something else she expected me to do, or should have). When we arrived, far ahead of the family, I found out there were some pretty steep stairs leading to the restaurant. I stood there in the rain for a minute trying to figure out what to do. Before I could decide, the doors flew open, two guys ran down the stairs, each grabbed a side of Taylor's wheelchair, and helped me lift her up the stairs. Now, this is in New York, considered one of the least friendly places in the

United States. But somehow, people knew what was needed, or even expected, and did it. Without being asked, without being told. They did it happily!

Why can't we all do this all the time? For people who maybe don't need as much help as Taylor, but maybe just a little help? Why can't we do this at our jobs? With our spouses and kids? With our parents? With our friends? With strangers?

People don't expect much, but it would be nice if there was an obvious need to be met that we all knew we could rely on those around us to do what they should to help.

I can't "opt out" with Taylor. We can't "opt out" with anyone.

CHAPTER 4

Accept Good Intentions

As mentioned in the previous chapter, based on the perspective I'm gaining from Taylor's point of view, we should all do what's expected to help. But there's a second part to that equation, we need to be accepting of people's help. This may sound odd to some, but many people refuse even the smallest amount of assistance. They're too proud, too self-confident, or don't want to owe anyone anything.

I know I was like that. I always wanted to do things myself. I "didn't need anything from anyone." My father and father-in-law would try to make helpful suggestions, and those suggestions would be offensive to me. People would occasionally offer a hand, and I would question their motives.

But once again, I looked to Taylor for perspective. Taylor is 100 percent reliant upon others. She never rejects assistance of any kind. She smiles as you help her through any of the hundreds of things she needs every day. Because if she did put up a fight, she wouldn't survive.

So why do so many of us think that we can do it on our own? How many of us could make our lives easier if we accepted help from those who wanted to help us achieve our goals, complete our tasks, or aid us in our daily choices?

Let those who are willing to help, do so. It will make them feel better, useful, and fulfilled. You may not only gain the assistance you need, you may also learn a tremendous amount in a short period of time by allowing them to participate in your life.

CHAPTER 5

Your Possessions
And their Effect on Your Happiness

Everyone strives to own things—cars, TVs, iPods, computers, clothes, houses, boats, etc. We all spend most of our lives working hard to earn the money to get things because this is what we've been programmed to do. This is what society tells us makes our lives full and happy.

I'm no different. I've owned BMWs, a Mercedes, a Corvette, a Hummer, a Lexus. We own two fully furnished homes and a condo. We owned boats, a jet ski, and all the toys you could imagine. Even my business is based on this desire for things, I sell diamonds for a living. But guess what? Not one of these things made me a happier person. Yes, they were fun to have, and I certainly enjoyed using them. But most of the time, something was wrong. They didn't work right, they became quickly outdated, or the technology toys were always broken. The cars and houses were expensive to insure and maintain.

With most possessions, the hassle outweighs the small joy they bring us. Most of us spend a lot of time complaining or being bothered by the problems our possessions cause or the time these problems take to resolve (think of time spent staring at a computer while it sits in a state of suspended animation).

But Taylor never complains about the things she has. From her perspective, if she gets to go in a ride in a convertible or a fast boat, she's had a thrill. If she gets a chance to watch a program or a video on a computer, she's enthralled. If she gets to listen to music on an iPod, she couldn't be happier. But if these things stop working, the ride ends, or the music or videos stop, she doesn't complain. She's happy for the experience she had and moves on. She looks to us for the next fun event.

Once you have your possessions, enjoy them to the best of your ability. If they stop working or stop bringing you joy, look around for what will bring you joy.

Your Possessions And their Effect on Your Happiness

That may not necessarily be a material possession. Because just like Taylor, the only real possessions we have are our minds and our bodies. That's it. Those are the only things we truly own and can bring us joy. By traditional standards, Taylor's two possessions don't operate as programmed. But yours do.

As we spend a lot of time hustling for things and then trying to use, maintain, repair, and insure these things to make us happy, we spend very little time caring for the only two possessions that matter. Most people would never treat their material possessions with as little attention as they do their minds and bodies. They just assume that they'll wake up in the morning and both those things will work fine.

Take care of the two possessions you really own and then work toward getting the material things you want. Having nice things isn't a crime. Spending all our time trying to earn money to buy them is.

CHAPTER 6

Don't Try to Control Others Because You Can't.

All of us feel frustration with others because from time to time; people can let us down. Running a business, I always felt let down—by my vendors, many of my employees, my advertisers, etc. Most people who know me through my businesses will tell you I was constantly trying to control how others behaved. I would rant and rave and try to teach a point. But after nineteen years of trying, there wasn't one person I was able to control.

I looked to Taylor. How could she teach me a lesson about this? Then it came to me—it was simply her existence. I'd like to control Taylor. To make her stand, walk, talk, eat, run, and play. But no matter what I do, I have absolutely no control over Taylor—her functioning or her achievements. She is who she is, and I must accept it because it's never going to change.

The perspective here is people are who they are, and you can't control them. They will do what they want or what they are capable of, and that's a hard lesson to learn.

Now, if you're a parent, you can set rules and boundaries and enforce those by rewarding your kids for doing things the way you'd like and punishing them for breaking the rules. If you have employees, you need a structure for them to follow. Again, if they excel, they should be rewarded, and if they fail (time and time again), they should be dismissed.

But don't get upset that people don't behave the way you want them to. Don't let it affect your mood for the day or your outlook for the week. Because the bottom line is, you have no control over others. You only have control over yourself. Knowing and remembering that will save you more stress than you can imagine.

CPSIA information can be obtained
at www.ICGtesting.com
Printed in the USA
BVHW092048090922
646659BV00006B/598

CHAPTER 7

Be True to Yourself

Many times, I find that people adjust to their surroundings. They try hard to impress others or act the way they think others want them to act. They don't let their true feelings be known or expressed for fear of how they will be perceived. I know I did this quite often in my twenties and thirties. I was always trying to adapt to the situation or the people I was around. Things weren't real, experiences weren't complete.

Taylor doesn't do this. If she's upset, she'll make a whining noise and throw up her hands in frustration. If she's bored, she'll act like she's nodding off. If she's sad, she cries. If she's interested in you, she'll lean in and try to listen to you. If she doesn't like you, she'll look away.

If she's happy, she laughs and smiles as big a smile as you'll ever see!

She doesn't know how to be different or try to adapt. She is who she is. That's not to say she expresses her feelings to the point of rudeness. She just simply *is* Taylor and acts the same way around everyone. She behaves the same no matter what. She expresses her opinions and feelings without being offensive.

Try and be considerate of others but never pretend to be someone you're not. Certainly let people know what you're really thinking, feeling, and wanting. Time is short, and there's no time to be someone you're not. You are unique and people need to know who you are.

Be True to Yourself

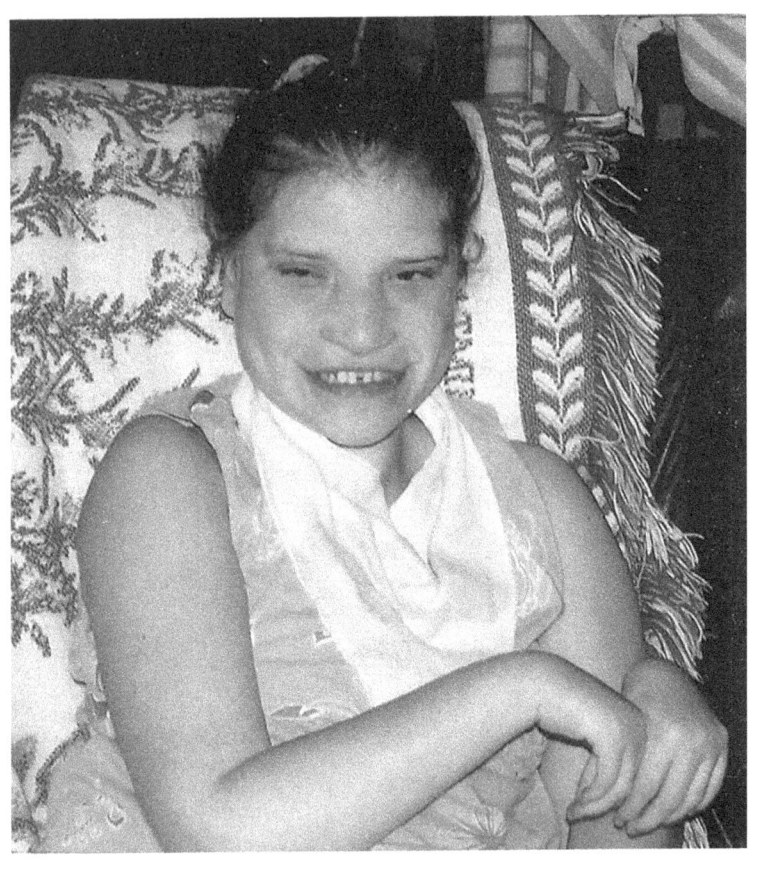

Taylor enjoying a laugh

Gaining Perspective, Lessons I'm Learning from Taylor

Taylor Excited for Christmas

Be True to Yourself

Taylor with her mom and sisters clockwise from left
Leslie, Tatum, Tiffany, Taylor and Jayda

Gaining Perspective, Lessons I'm Learning from Taylor

Taylor and the family celebrating
Thanksgiving in Manhattan

CHAPTER 8

Remember People's Names: It's Really Important.

I always said I was one of those guys who "can remember faces but not names." Most of the time when we meet people, we're trying so hard to impress them and put our best foot forward that we don't even hear the other person's name! But there is one thing that Taylor responds to more than anything else—her name! We don't know how much she understands, but one thing is clear—she responds to her name being called. She smiles, looks toward the source, and gets excited. Sometimes I'll repeat her name ten times to her just to watch her happy reaction.

Upon gaining this perspective, I really started trying hard to remember people's names. If I forgot, the next time I would see them, I would apologize and ask for it again. I would explain that I was trying hard to be good with names. When I would see these people, I would go out of my way to not only greet them, but greet them by name. You know what? I would get the same happy reaction that I got from Taylor.

Yes, there were "filters" of sophistication there. But I got attention, I got smiles, and I got pleasant reactions. People who formerly would just greet me with a "Hey, how are you?" would now start saying, "Hey, Dave, how's it going?" It was more personal, more pleasant, and a more enjoyable interaction.

Kids love it when an adult remembers their name. I try hardest with them. So many kids are pushed into the background that they light up when an adult treats them as someone worth remembering, someone who's important.

Go out of your way to learn people's names and then call them by it, even if the person is a casual acquaintance. It will make such a difference in their reaction to you that you will both be enriched in your daily lives.

CHAPTER 9

Perspective on Diet

Food is necessary to survive. We all know this. But eating food has become a national pastime. Almost every social event is centered around food. Most of the food we consume doesn't provide us with the basic healthful nutrients we need to survive, let alone allow us to thrive. In addition, how many of us complain about the poor taste of the food we eat, the quality, lack of freshness, and even the poor service we receive when dining out?

But none of this is an issue for Taylor. Her muscle control is so poor that she cannot consume enough food to live. At age four and a half, she weighed only twenty-three pounds, and she had a feeding tube permanently installed in her stomach.

Taylor's entire diet consists of liquid nutrients. She gets exactly what she needs to survive and thrive. She never has to worry about poor-tasting food nor does she ever complain about it. She never has to worry if the things she's consuming are good for her or not, as my wife and I only give her the prescribed formula. She never complains that the service is bad—she's happy to be fed.

Learn to know what your body needs to thrive. It's not complicated: fresh fruits and vegetables, whole grains, and lean meat. All these things are what you need for a healthy body. If you want to take it one step further, try a liquid diet of healthy protein shakes or smoothies. Do it for a meal, a day, two days, or even a week at a time. Make sure you're getting the calories you need to function at your peak. You'll find you feel stronger, lighter, and more alert.

The next time you eat solid food or dine out after just consuming liquid, you more than likely won't complain about the food or the service. It will seem like you're eating the best food in the world in the best restaurant in the world. Your perspective on food will most certainly change.

CHAPTER 10

Watch What You Do to Yourself

Drug and alcohol use continues to persist in spite of the warnings about the consequences to your health. They continue to be used, even though they can come with dire legal penalties for use or resulting from their overuse (driving under the influence, etc.).

I certainly learned how to enjoy a cocktail or two as an adult. And I still do occasionally. But when it started to seem like I needed a drink to have a good time with my friends, I once again looked to Taylor for advice. What would Taylor think of drugs and alcohol if she were suddenly able to walk, talk, run, or interact with others? Would she find it ridiculous that people who have so many abilities and opportunities to perform at peak levels consume multiple substances to render themselves less than fully capable?

If suddenly able to speak, would she drink something that would jumble her thoughts and limit her capacity to fully communicate her ideas? I'm fairly certain she wouldn't. So why do we? Drugs not only limit your ability to do the things you want to do in the short term but possibly for the rest of your life. Drinking, if done at all, should be done in moderation, to relax but not to render yourself helpless and unable to function.

You have so many talents and interesting points of view. Don't neutralize those gifts with chemicals.

CHAPTER 11

Experience Love

How many of us obsess about a love lost? How many times do we hear about a love gone wrong and the heartache it caused? How many times do we hear about someone who stays in a relationship for convenience or money long after the love has gone away? How many of us take our loved ones for granted? The people who mean the most to us (spouses, children, brothers, sisters, and parents) get the least of our attention and see the worst of us because for some odd reason, the people we hardly know get our best manners.

I know this happened with me. I often put off things with my kids because there would always be more time. My wife would hear my rants about my day, and over time, it caused her to shut me out and consider leaving me. I assumed that love was there to stay, no matter what—boy, was I wrong.

But Taylor will never experience love the way you and I can. I hope she knows how much her family loves her. I'm sure she can tell when we spend time with her. But she isn't able to express her love for people. If she could, she certainly wouldn't use angry words with those who love her and whom she loves.

But saddest of all, she'll never experience romantic love. She'll never know the amazing feeling of a first kiss or the rush of knowing someone she likes is in love with her. She'll never have a date, a boyfriend, or a husband. She'll never have kids. These are all sources of deep love that Taylor will never experience and you can—possibly multiple times!

So don't complain about a lost love. You experienced the deep love while it was there and, in time, will most likely experience it again. If you're feeling heartache, it's only because you also got to experience the great feeling of being in love. If you're with someone you don't truly love, it's not fair to either of you that you stay in that relationship for convenience. You owe it to both of you to find real love and enjoy it to the fullest. If you're as fortunate as I am to be in love with your spouse of many years, make sure to let that person know on a regular basis how much he or she means to you and how much you love them.

Last but not least, understand what an incredible gift it is to experience the love of your own children. Never take the time you have with them for granted, and make all the time possible to enjoy them and participate in the things that are important to them. These things are so special, and it's important to realize what a true reward deep love really is in your life.

CHAPTER 12

Encourage Others

So often, it's our natural reaction to look for the negative in the efforts, goals, and plans of others. We frequently discourage people from reaching for their dreams because we feel they're too farfetched. We think we're helping them by keeping them on a safe path. Why do we always try to focus on the things people can't do? Why do we tell them we think they can't do something? Why don't we encourage them to focus on the things they can do?

I know with Taylor, all we do is encourage her. The things she is able to accomplish may seem trivial to most, but when she is reaching for a toy, trying to roll over, working on standing with the aid of a stander, we do nothing but encourage her strongly.

Can you imagine Taylor attempting to reach for a toy (one of the things she's most proud of) and us yelling, "Give it up, you'll never get it," or "I wouldn't try that if I were you—what makes you think you're so special?" So why in the world would we do this with anyone else? Almost every day, we are told what we can't do instead of what we can do. Almost every day, we tell someone else what we think they can't do. Why is this?

Quit listening to the negative people in your life who will stop at nothing to keep you from your goals and desires. More importantly, don't only stop yourself from discouraging others, go that extra step and encourage people when you see them trying something new, reaching for their goals, or just expressing a dream to you. Focus and get excited about the things people can do and want to do, and don't focus on what can't be done.

CHAPTER 13

Learn Patience

I've always struggled with patience. Anyone who knows me will tell you I'm one of the least patient people they know. I can't stand the thought of burning up valuable time doing nothing while waiting for something to take place. I've always been this way. But as many times as I've tried, I've never found that my ranting, coaxing, and cajoling managed to speed up a situation where I found myself waiting.

In the midst of writing this book, I found myself stuck in an airport with my wife, Leslie. It was a tiny little airport with no restaurants, bookstores, shops, or any other kinds of diversions to make the time pass more quickly. As the airline employees ignored us and gave us erroneous "updates" every hour or so (over the course of a three-plus-hour wait), I found myself getting madder and madder. Leslie looked at me and said, "Where is the chapter in your book on this?" I thought for a while and tried to figure out how Taylor would "advise me" on dealing with a situation like this.

The simple fact is Taylor exercises more patience than anyone I know. Her entire life is one long wait. She's not able to do anything for herself. Anytime she wants something to happen, she has to wait for it. She has no choice. When things happen, they happen, and she is ready to go.

Her life is not so dissimilar from ours. Because so many things are out of our control, we simply have no choice but to wait. There's no amount of action that can speed up ninety-nine percent of the actions of those for whom we're waiting.

So it's up to us to exercise patience in every waiting scenario. Taylor does it for every single event in her life. We certainly can learn to be patient when we have no other choice.

CHAPTER 14

Exceed Your Limitations Every Day!

This is the final lesson we all need to learn from Taylor. If just one percent of the people reading this guide on gaining perspective from Taylor take this to heart, their world and ours could become full of amazing accomplishments and achievements. Every day, try to accomplish something you know you can't do yet or have failed at before. *Every day*.

There are so many things in life that we want to achieve whether it's getting in better shape, finishing that degree, opening a business, starting a family, buying a home, etc. There are literally millions of things that people want to accomplish but are afraid to try. They're afraid because they have failed before—maybe more than once. Or the obstacles seem insurmountable because they had no experience in their area of interest.

But every single morning, Taylor tries to sit up in bed to greet the day. Every single morning, she reaches for the sky and tries with all her might to sit up to see me or her mom or even her TV. And every morning, she rises a tiny bit—some mornings an inch or two and others, a centimeter. On her best day, she rose almost halfway. But you know what also happens every morning? She falls back down. In twenty-one years (at the time of this writing), Taylor has attempted this feat every single morning. And every single morning for twenty-one years, she's failed.

Now, she must know that she hasn't been able to do this. But every single day, I see the bravest person I know trying again to do something she hasn't accomplished in twenty-one years of daily failure. Maybe she doesn't know, and that's even better. She just wakes up with the belief she can do it, tries, fails and thinks, "Well, I'll try again tomorrow." Then she wakes up the next day without the memory of failure and has no fear in trying again.

How many of us are that brave or persistent? How many are that determined to reach for their goals? I would hazard a guess that the answer is none of us. But we each have this ability. We each have the opportunity of a new day, every twenty-four hours, to try again.

Please try every day to accomplish something you deeply desire. It can be the smallest of dreams or the grandest plan ever set forth by mankind. What are you waiting for? Today is here, and we haven't tried. Or, we tried once or twice, failed, and gave up.

We have to keep trying every day whether or not we reach our dreams and goals; we still know that our lives can be fulfilled, just as Taylor's is, by the daily effort of reaching for our dreams. Simply knowing that the daily effort is good enough will give you the perspective to enjoy every endeavor.